Charles Stanhope, Charles Hawtrey

A Letter to Earl Stanhope

on the subject of the Test, as objected to in a pamphlet recommended by

His Lordship

Charles Stanhope, Charles Hawtrey

A Letter to Earl Stanhope
on the subject of the Test, as objected to in a pamphlet recommended by His Lordship

ISBN/EAN: 9783337091835

Printed in Europe, USA, Canada, Australia, Japan

Cover: Foto ©Andreas Hilbeck / pixelio.de

More available books at **www.hansebooks.com**

A

L E T T E R

TO

EARL STANHOPE,

ON THE

SUBJECT OF THE TEST,

AS OBJECTED TO IN A PAMPHLET

RECOMMENDED BY HIS LORDSHIP.

———————

OXFORD PRINTED;

AND SOLD BY J. FLETCHER, IN THE TURLE; AND

MESS. RIVINGTON, ST. PAUL'S CHURCH - YARD,

LONDON.

M DCC LXXXIX.

A

LETTER

T O

EARL STANHOPE, &c.

My Lord,

AN obfcure perfon, unknown to your Lordfhip or to the world, begs leave to addrefs you on the fubject of a Pamphlet lately publifhed, and which hath been fo highly honoured with your Lordfhip's approbation, that you have recommended it as the beft pamphlet that has been publifhed upon religion for a whole century. The title of the pamphlet is, " The Right of the " Proteftant Diffenters to a complete Tole- " ration afferted;" but if the pamphlet it- felf hath nothing in it more worthy of approbation than this title, it is to be feared your Lordfhip hath been a little too fan- guine in your recommendation. Probably

the

the author made a little miftake here, and meant to have faid, " The *Claim* of the Pro- " teftant Diffenters, &c. juftified." If, however, he did not, he certainly has un- dertaken a moft Herculean tafk. It is no- thing lefs than to prove that the Diffenters have a *right* to what others have a fuperior right to with-hold from them. A right to a toleration is a contradiction in terms, for a toleration muft be a matter of favour or courtefy, and not a matter of right. If a toleration is not a matter of favour or cour- tefy, then no man hath a right either to grant or withhold it, and then what is the author pleading for? is he pleading for a grant which he hath without its being granted? Strange wildnefs this! It is very much to be feared, my Lord, we fhall find this admirable pamphlet not to be the very beft pamphlet that has been publifhed upon religion for a whole century.

It is a common cafe, my Lord, for perfons who can difcern merit where there is none, not to be able to difcover faults where they are moft notorious. That the Diffenters have a right to thofe privileges which the law has given them is beyond a doubt, and thus they have a right to fuch privileges and exemptions as they enjoy by the act of to- leration,

leration, but that they have a right to privileges and exemptions which the law hath not granted them cannot be afferted with any the fmalleft degree of truth or propriety. No man in fociety hath a right to privileges till the law of that fociety hath given them its fanction. More privileges than he enjoys he may indeed lay claim to, but right he can have none to them, becaufe the right is in the fociety either to grant or to withold them.

If the Diffenters have a right, why do they not exert it ? who is it witholds it from them ? their right, if they have any, ·muft be fanctioned by the laws ; let them then appeal to thefe laws, and act under them, and they need not fear but the laws will protect them in it from any interruption ; but if they have not the laws on their fide, they moft affuredly have not right, for right in fociety is eftablifhed only by law.

But the title and fubject of this fo admired a performance is open to objection upon another account. The author fays, the Diffenters have a right to a *complete* toleration. What does the writer mean by a complete toleration ? does he mean that the Diffenters ought to have all the fame privileges as thofe who are not Diffenters ? but this would not

A 3 be

be a toleration but an establishment, so here your Lordship's pamphletteer blunders again; for, if this was his meaning, he ought not to have used the word toleration. But let us suppose this was not his meaning, and that by the word toleration he means nothing beyond what it signifies in its constant usage. Then the question is, what is to be understood by a complete toleration? words not usually combined together, and which, though they may have some determinate sense in the author's intention, yet in the reader's apprehension are scarcely intelligible.

Whoever is tolerated is completely tolerated in the instance for which the toleration is granted, because an incomplete toleration in the instance for which it is granted is no toleration at all. Now most certain it is that the Dissenters are tolerated in the free exercise of their religion; they have houses wherein they meet together; teachers who direct them; they have a discipline, and rules, and laws of their own, by which they govern themselves unrestrained or controlled; and, in their religious tenets and opinions, let them be ever so wild or absurd, or even false, they are tolerated in the free enjoyment of them. Now if the Dissenters are thus tolerated,

tolerated, wherein, my Lord, is the defect in this toleration? how, or in what inftance are they curbed or reftrained in their confciences, or indeed what can poffibly be added to this toleration to render it more than it is. Uninterrupted they enjoy their religious opinions, and without interruption they are fuffered to worfhip the Deity in the way which feemeth right to them in their own eyes. Would they have more than the free and uninterrupted enjoyment of their religious opinions and practices? What can that *more* be? for, after having granted them ALL that is meant by a religious toleration, any addition to it becomes impoffible. Thus, my Lord, we reafon unavoidably from the title of this curious pamphlet, and begin to fufpect, that by the word toleration the writer means what the word toleration does not fignify, and upon looking into the pamphlet we are very fully confirmed in this fufpicion; for inftead of ftating that the Proteftant Diffenters have not the full and undifturbed enjoyment of their religious opinions and practices; inftead of pointing out what the obftacles are which hinder it, and which ought to be removed, it does not appear that there is one fingle fyllable faid

upon

upon the subject throughout the whole pamphlet.

The first forty-eight pages are employed in a dry uninterefting detail, which he calls a hiftory of the teft laws, and the remaining fifty-one pages, if they have any tendency, tend to prove that Proteftant Diffenters ought to enjoy the fame civil privileges and emoluments as thofe who are not Diffenters. But what hath this to do, my Lord, with toleration? are not Diffenters tolerated becaufe the laws of our country have provided that the mayor of a corporation fhall be a member of the eftablifhment. The laws have provided not only that the inferior magiftrate but that the chief magiftrate fhall be a member of the eftablifhment, and are the Diffenters not tolerated becaufe a Diffenter cannot be king of England? If there is a defect in the toleration becaufe a Diffenter may not be mayor of a corporation, there is a defect in it becaufe he may not be king of England, and it is not at all improbable but that your Lordfhip's friend, *the Layman,* thinks as much; however, he muft think again before he will think right upon this fubject. A religious toleration is a toleration for the purpofes of religion only, and is totally detached from every confideration of

lucrative

lucrative offices in or under the state; and therefore all that the Layman urges concerning the right of Protestant Dissenters to enjoy lucrative places, is just so much of nothing at all to his purpose, which, as his title informs us, is to assert the right of Protestant Dissenters to a compleat toleration. Suppose, my Lord, for the sake of a little amusement, we alter the title of this most admirable pamphlet, and endeavour to bring it a little nearer to the subject of which it treats, will it not run then something to this purpose? *The right of Protestant Dissenters to the enjoyment of those places of trust and emolument which by the laws are appropriated to members only of the establishment.* But in what, my Lord, must this right commence? not in in the laws, for the laws are in direct opposition to it; not antecedent to the laws, for the *test*, as the writer himself acknowledges, was long before any Protestants had separated from the establishment; and therefore we must look for the origin of this right only in those days (Pt. 2. ch. 1), when man was in a state of nature; i. e. when he had the happiness of being ornamented with one of lord Monboddo's long tails. Facts, my Lord, never can be established by arguments drawn merely from speculation. If
the

the Diffenters have a right it is the right of *Diffenters quâ tales,* and not fimply as they are men, and therefore any arguments drawn from the rights of mankind in a fpeculative ftate of nature do not by any means apply. The Diffenters are perfons formed out of a body of men who voluntarily withdrew themfelves, in part, from that fociety to which they did belong, as not chufing to comply with all the terms which it did pre-fcribe; all the right therefore which they appear to have in the cafe is, a right of being admitted again if they chufe to comply with the fociety's terms. But it would be ftrange indeed if they had a right of admiffion to all the privileges and emoluments of the fociety, not only without a compliance with its terms, but in direct oppofition to them. If the Diffenters' claim of right, as ftated by your lordfhip's friend, the pamphletteer, is juft and well-founded, all fociety in the world is at an end; for in the very idea of a fociety is included a compliance with the laws by which it is governed and maintained. De-fire your friend, my Lord, to confider a little thenature of fociety, not as it is in the con-ceits of fpeculation, but as it exifts in fact, and then let him fay what poffible right a man can have to the profits and advantages

of

of that fociety (and a kingdom is a fociety only upon a larger fcale) with whofe terms of admiffion and laws he does not chufe to comply.

It is not the intention of thefe pages to examine minutely the feveral tautologies of this writer: his unneceffary quotations; his quotations upon quotations from journals, fpeeches, &c. and which, as to the point in queftion, have very little or no relation at all. It will be fufficient to obviate the main intention of his pamphlet, and to take notice of fome of the moft obnoxious parts. Let us begin with the following:

"Falfe foundations (faith the writer, p. "53) are naturally accompanied by fophifti- "cal inferences." He doth not exprefs himfelf in the cleareft manner; however we will take it as he gives it us. Now, p. 52, his words are, "If I am a good member of the "civil fociety, I ftand upon an equal footing "with every other member, confidered as "fuch; and it is no offence to government, "if I behave with duty and refpect to it, "that I worfhip God in a manner fomewhat "different from my neighbours; nor is it a "fufficient reafon for excluding me from all "publick fervice and truft. Incapacities of "the nature in queftion fhould be inflicted "as

" as punifhments for crimes againft the ftate;
" and Proteftant Diffenters ought to be no
" longer liable to *any punifhment*, fince, by
" the laws of England, non-conformity has
" ceafed to be a crime." On what fort of
foundation is this built? affuredly on a
foundation which will not fupport its fu-
perftructure. If I am, fays he, a good
member of the civil fociety. But, my Lord,
if you pleafe, we will leave out the word
good, and the confequences will be juft the
fame, for he that really is a member of a
fociety is undoubtedly entitled to the privileges which belong to the members of that
fociety. Now it is effential to every fociety
in the world, that the perfons who are its
members fhould have complied with the
terms of admiffion into it, and that they
fhould fubmit, as far as they extend, to be
governed by its laws; none but perfons of
this defcription being entitled to fhare in the
privileges and emoluments of fuch fociety.
Whoever then is fuch a member as this of
the civil fociety is not excluded from all public fervice and truft, even though he fhould
not be a good member, but only an occafional
conformift. What then is the writer aiming
at? He is not excluded if he will comply
with the terms; and if he does not chufe

to

to comply with them, whofe fault is that ? The civil fociety exercifeth no authority upon this occafion more than is exercifed by every fociety upon earth; and, indeed, without the exercife of which it could not poffibly be a fociety. Therefore in this cafe there is no wrong, no hardfhip, no punifhment inflicted upon Proteftant Diffenters, and confequently their complaint is without caufe.

But perhaps it may be faid, that the *Civil Society* of a country is not of the nature of thofe formed focieties of which it is at a man's option whether he will become a member of them or not. A man is born, without any option of his own, a member of the civil fociety; but, obferve, of the civil fociety already formed and eftablifhed, in which it is provided, that all its members, indifferently, fhall fhare in its fupport and protection, but that fuch only as fhall have the requifite qualification fhall be employed in the public fervice and truft. If the Diffenter hath that qualification he may be employed as freely as any one that is not a Diffenter; if he hath it not is the civil fociety to blame upon this account, or doth the fociety inflict any punifhment upon him for not having it ? By what right then doth he complain ? If he hath a right of complaint, fo hath every day

day labourer a much greater right, who is born a member of the civil fociety, as truly as the Diffenter, and yet, as not being a freeholder (which it neither is nor ever was in his power to have remedied), is not fuffered to give his vote in the election of a member of parliament; fo likewife is the freeholder, who, let his perfonal property be ever fo great, ftill is excluded from being a member of the Houfe of Commons if his freehold be not of the prefcribed value; and fo likewife in a variety of other inftances. But no man ever yet heard that thefe, and fuch like limitations were confidered as punifhments, which, at the fame time, they muft be if the Diffenters' complaints are juft.

But the writer fays, " It is no offence to " government if he behaves with duty " and refpect to it; that he worfhips God in " a manner fomewhat different from his " neighbour." Neither doth government take offence at it, but freely fuffers him to do it with impunity. " Nor is it (faith he) " a fufficient reafon for excluding me from " all public fervice and truft." Here, contrary to fact, it is fuggefted that Diffenters are *excluded* from all public fervice and truft. They are NOT excluded, places of public fervice are as open to them as to any others

of

of the community. To none are they open,
be he *Tros Tyriufve*, who hath not the
requifite qualification; and therefore, in
this refpect, there is not the leaft degree of
difference between a perfon that is, and a
perfon that is not a Diffenter; neither of
them is admiffible except qualified as by the
wifdom of the laws it is required they fhould
be, and of courfe the above fuggeftion hath
no truth in it.

The concluding paffage in the citation already made is laughable enough : " Incapa-
" cities of the nature in queftion fhould be in-
" flicted as punifhments for crimes againft the
" ftate; and Proteftant Diffenters ought to be
" no longer liable to *any punifhment*, fince, by
" the laws of England, non-conformity has
" ceafed to be a crime." And fo, my Lord,
becaufe non-conformity has ceafed to be a
crime, therefore your Lordfhip's friend ought
not to be hanged when he is guilty of any
thing that deferves it. This is pretty and
amufing; however, let us take the matter as
moft probably the author meant it fhould be
taken ; i. e. that Diffenters ought not to be
liable to any punifhment on account of their
non-conformity ; and let it be granted that
they ought not, doth it therefore follow that
they ought to be exempted from thofe re-
ftrictions

ſtrictions which are laid upon all in general,
without exception ; or can thoſe reſtrictions,
with any manner of truth, be ſtiled puniſhments whch operate upon the whole community ; moſt aſſuredly they cannot. The
Teſt laws are general, and compliance with
them is required from all ; they do not more
particularly affect the Diſſenter than the reſt
of the community ; and therefore by no rule
of ſenſe or right reaſon can they be ſtiled
puniſhments particularly inflicted on the Diſſenters. It ever was, even from the days of
the Druids, the conſtant uninterrupted prac-
tice of the kingdom, that offices of public
ſervice and truſt ſhould be in the hands of
thoſe only who profeſſed the eſtabliſhed religion, let that religion have been what it
might ; and whenever it ſo happened that
either through fraud or violence theſe offices
were gotten into other hands, the conſe-
quence generally was a ſubverſion and total
overthrow of the eſtabliſhed religion ; and
that ſuch would be the event if the Diſſenters ſhould be admitted to places of power
and truſt there needs no ſpirit of prophecy
to aſſure us. Religion, my Lord, is the
deareſt concern of mankind, and the Diſſenters would ſoon convince us how dear it
was to them, by making us all bend, as far
as

as their power fhould reach, to their yoke. There was a time when they were in power, and their language then was, that a toleration was eftablifhing iniquity by law; when they are again in power they will doubtlefs again refume the fame language, for the fpirit and principle of their religion will dictate it to them.

It is true, your Lordfhip's friend affects to difclaim every thing of this kind. As he reprefents matters, the Diffenters (p. 58) are the trueft friends and protectors of the eftablifhment, and have faved it from being brought to defolation ; in which, if he believes himfelf, it is well, but it is imagined very few will be inclined to give him credit. We well know when the Diffenters defolated us, and our churches even at this day bear rueful marks of it ; but when they faved us from defolation, if known to themfelves, is totally unknown to us. At the revolution they certainly did it not, although he wifhes to have it thought they did ; their conduct at that period was daftardly and unmeritorious in the higheft degree ; they had juft before addreffed, and flattered, and cringed to James the Second, perfuading him that he might depend upon all the affiftance they could give him ; but when the ftorm began

B   to

roll, and the throne to totter under the poor infatuated monarch, they then deserted him, joined themselves to his opponents, and now make a merit of this junction, which (as they had deserted their king) was the only thing they could do.

When James was upon the throne, and Popery threatened to become triumphant, the Diffenters, says your Lordfhip's friend, p. 19, found an afylum in the bofom of the prerogative. Happy mortals! and how did they find this afylum? the reader fhall be told. James, for the purpofe of effectually fubverting the church of England, and eftablifhing Popery in its room, was determined upon the abolition of the Teft. In thefe meafures the Diffenters concurred with him, and then found, and if the overruling providence of God had not directed otherwife, would have ftill continued to find, an afylum in the bofom of the Prerogative, but at the fame time in the downfall of the Church of England.

When James failed, at leaft, when the profpect became fo overclouded that there was no room to hope for fuccefs, " In this " extremity (faith the pamphleteer) they did " not forget the precarious tenure by which " they held this indulgence ;" *i. e.* they faw
that

that James would not be able any longer to
afford them an afylum; and what did they
then? they " preferred the chance of a legal
" toleration to fervile dependence on the will
" of a prince." But the king was, or they
certainly knew would be oufted, confequently
James would have no will on which they
might fervilely depend; how therefore was
it poffible for them to fhew that preference
which is here fpoken of? Hath not your
friend, my Lord, deviated a little in this
inftance from the ftrait line of truth and
matter of fact? There was no poffibility of
any preference being given in the cafe.
James was no longer able to protect or affift
them, and without his affiftance they were
unable to cope with the Church of England;
nay, with it they had failed of fuccefs, therefore they had nothing left them but to ac-
quiefce, in hopes that when things were
fettled there might be a chance of a legal
toleration, which at the fame time they did by
no means deferve.

The principles of the Diffenters are and
ever will be hoftile to the Church of England; and, as we have already feen, they
will combine even with the Papifts for its
overthrow; and moreover, even at this hour,
they have the confidence to denominate fuch

a com-

a combination " a finding an afylum from
" their perfecutors in the bofom of the pre-
" rogative ; and yet this writer tells us, that
" the modern Diffenters entertain no opi-
" nions hoftile to church or ftate." Is it
poffible for them to ufe fuch language as the
above, and not entertain opinions hoftile to
the Church? Their opinions at this hour
áre the fame as when they combined with
James for the overthrow of the church;
and, whenever an opportunity offers, there
cannot be a doubt (if we may judge from
the language of your Lordfhip's friend) they
will combine again for the fame purpofe.

It is well worthy of obfervation the viru-
lence with which this writer expreffeth himfelf againft the friends of the eftablifhment.
He tells us, p. 58, " The defence of the
" Teft laws is even now refted upon their
" being a weapon of defence to guard the
" eftablifhment from the attacks of thofe
" *who are prepared to catch at every opportu-*
" *nity to do it harm* ;" and referring to a
fermon of bifhop Hallifax, he proceeds, " Do
" Proteftant Diffenters catch at every oppor-
" tunity to do harm to the eftablifhment?
" The right reverend prelate feems to be as
" little acquainted with the hiftory of his
" own country as with *the true fpirit of Chrif-*
                                        " *tianity.*"

" *tianity*." What almost could any man say worse, or with blacker malignity, of a Christian Bishop than this? It is true his Lordship needs no vindication from so infamous a charge, and which is so notoriously known to be false, the notoriety of its being false is vindication sufficient; but it serves to shew what manner of spirit your Lordship's friend is of. Again, speaking of the Bishop, p. 59, he says, " Let him enjoy in " security and peace his own situation, but " let him not become an advocate for per- " secution, or a traducer of the oppressed." What can be in the head of this man, or what is he dreaming of? Name the persecution that the good Bishop is an advocate for; name the oppressed party that he is traducing. O my noble Earl! how can you be an advocate for a writer who thus, either in folly or madness scattereth his firebrands at random?

As he hath treated the present very worthy Bishop of St. Asaph, so, in like manner doth he treat the prime minister, Mr. Pitt, p. 93, he tells us " the Dissenters " had a claim to the gratitude of the minister, " in whose elevation they had born a most dis- " tinguished part." This piece of intelligence is too much above my comprehension to be

able

able to make any thing of it, as I never yet heard that the Diffenters were the perfons who appointed Mr. Pitt to be the King's prime minifter. To be fure this honeft man muft have fomething in his head, but what I fhall not pretend to conjecture. However, he proceeds: " Their favourite minifter " (faith he) difclaiming indeed perfecution " in words, admitted the whole extent of " its principle, and flood foremoft in the " ranks againft them;" *i. e.* at the time when they failed in their application for a repeal of the Teft laws ; fo that here we fee even their favourite minifter, as they chufe to call him, muft not efcape the obloquy of the Diffenters if he is a friend to the eftablifhment. He is, it feems, a fhameful prevaricator, difclaiming perfecution in his words, but ftanding foremoft in the ranks among their perfecutors. The minifter needs no vindication from this obloquy; it is known to the whole kingdom that Mr. Pitt is no perfecutor ; it is known likewife to the whole kingdom that the Diffenters are not perfecuted. But it feems the minifter is not only a prevaricator, but a ftranger likewife to found argument; for, p. 95, " One of the " arguments much preffed againft the Dif- " fenters was, *the danger arifing from innova-* " *tion.*

" *tion.* This argument in the mouth of a
" ftatefman hardly deferves a ferious an-
" fwer ;" and yet the argument is a good
one, let your mode of anfwering be what it
will ; however, let us fee what the anfwer
to it is. " A minifter (he fays) ought not
" fight the battles of a Quixote, nor ought
" he rafhly expofe his country to danger ;
" but it is the duty of his fituation to put
" the public tranquility even to fome hazard
" in favour of a change where the good to
" be expected confiderably exceeds the evil
" to be feared." Here then the minifter's
argument, which hardly deferved a ferious
anfwer, is acknowledged to be good, *inno-*
vation is hazardous. A change could not be
effected without putting the public tranquility to fome hazard ; but it was the duty of
the minifter (he fays) to put it to this hazard where the good to be expected confiderably exceeded the evil to be feared ; which
in the prefent inftance was not the cafe, for the
good arifing from it would be the admitting
of Meffieurs the Diffenters to lucrative places
of truft, and the evils to be feared were the
fubverfion and total overthrow of the conftitution ; fo that the minifter's argument,
notwithftanding the contemptuous manner

B 4   in

in which this writer hath treated it, is valid, firm, and unanſwerable.

From abuſe and obloquy the writer proceeds to his peroration, and a flaming one it is, p. 97, " Let not the Proteſtant Diſſenters " put their truſt in king, miniſter, or pre- " lates, but let them confide in THEIR OWN " EXERTIONS, the juſtneſs of their cauſe, " and the *generoſity of the nation*." And again, p. 99, " Should king, miniſter, and " prelates be arrayed againſt them, let them " not ſhrink from the conteſt." This language, my Lord, it muſt be owned, is very plain and undiſguiſed, but how far it is calculated for conciliating to the Diſſenters the generoſity of the nation, may, I think, without much difficulty, be eaſily aſcertained. Little indeed can they be entitled to the generoſity of a nation which they are thus labouring to throw into confuſion ; and if the Diſſenters think otherwiſe, it is imagined, they will find themſelves much, very much miſtaken. In the threat likewiſe thrown out againſt the members of the preſent Houſe of Commons there is a degree of inſolence almoſt unpardonable. They who have voted for the repeal of the Teſt laws may go down with confidence to their conſtituents ; but ſuch as have not, and ſuch

he

he is pleafed to ftile *obftinate advocates for perfecution*, can have no claim to their affiftance. Fine language this to be ufed towards any member of the Houfe of Commons when acting in his fenatorial capacity, and much more when ufed towards the majority of that houfe. The refutation of this moft illiberal charge is, that the author of it hath not as yet had his ears nailed to the pillory, which certainly would have been the cafe, or worfe, if the prefent Houfe of Commons had been the barbarous perfecutors which he is pleafed to reprefent them to be. How, my Lord, will you reconcile this virulent abufe of the friends of the eftablifhment with the writer's frequent declaration, that the modern Diffenters are not hoftile to the eftablifhment? If they are not hoftile to the eftablifhment, why are they fo hoftile to its advocates and fupporters? Can this want any comment? The language of infolence and abufe never can proceed but from the moft hoftile difpofition, nor the language of defiance but from thofe who are meditating the overthrow of thofe whom they defy. It is to be hoped this man's voice is not the voice of the Diffenters in general, if it is it muft lower them exceedingly in the opinion of thofe who are well-wifhers to the

con-

conſtitution of their country, a conſtitution that is the envy and admiration of other countries, and that ſtands unequalled in the annals of the world. Let us, my Lord, attend a little to it, and more eſpecially be-cauſe your friend has attached to his pamphlet a letter of Sir William Meredith, wherein the conſtitution is repreſented to be ſo very different from what it really is.

The worthy Baronet's letter it ſeems was in anſwer to one from a Diſſenting miniſter at Liverpool, and its ſentiments perhaps thoſe of an occaſional conformiſt with the ſentiments of the perſon to whom he addreſſed himſelf. His words are theſe : " All Pro-" teſtants agree in this one point, to ſup-" port our preſent conſtitution as a republic, " under the adminiſtration of a king, whoſe " title is ſacred while he preſerves our laws, " but forfeited if- he attempts to break " them." If theſe words expreſſed the real ſentiments of the writer he was undoubtedly very much miſtaken, and very much a ſtranger to the real conſtitution of the Engliſh go-vernment.

The Engliſh conſtitution neither is nor ever was republican. Its baſis is monarchy from the earlieſt origin to which we can trace it ; and the preſent government is a monarchy ſo
tempered

tempered, fo providentially blended with the Hierarchical, Ariftocratical, and Democratical forms of government, as to form one complete whole, wherein both governors and governed are held under the reftraint as well as protection of the laws; wherein the fubject enjoyeth the fullnefs of his liberty without licentioufnefs, and the monarch his powers and his honours without being arbitrary. Gradually framed by the hand of ages, it is now fettled into a moft truly venerable ftructure, wherein is treafured up all that is valuable in every form of government known upon the face of the earth. Long, very long, even to the lateft pofterity may it remain flourifhing and firmly fixed on its bafis, undifturbed either by popular or fanatical madnefs, and unopprefled by the iron hand of tyranny or power.

Now from the above fhort reprefentation of our invaluable conftitution it is evident, that all attempts at innovation cannot but be attended with danger in the extreme; and that compliance with the wifhes of Diffenters from the eftablifhment would be to rifk the total overthrow of the whole fabric; for the idea of the Diffenters, with regard to the conftitution (if Sir William Meredith has truly given it) is entirely different from that which

which is here expreffed. It is the idea of a
republic exercifing its authority over the monarchy, faying to their king, you fhall not
tranfgrefs our laws, or you have tranfgreffed
them, and we will place another in your
room. But this is not the Englifh conftitution ; there is nothing of Democratical ftern-
nefs in it, it is all mild and even, and regu-
lated throughout, fo that any irregularity in
one part may be inftantly and neceffarily cor-
rected by the movements of the other parts,
without diforder or confufion; but in the
Diffenter's idea, any irregularity happening
(and irregularities will fometimes happen in
all human governments) there would be no
remedy but in wild uproar, and the unreftrained rage of the people; and to fuch a
miferably perturbed ftate as this would the
conftitution, in all probability, be foon reduced were the innovating plan in favour of
the Diffenters to take place.

For let it be obferved that the repeal of
Teft laws is not objected to merely on account of the ecclefiaftical eftablifhment, but
on account of the *whole conftitution* to which
the principles of the Diffenters are as oppofite as they are to the ecclefiaftical eftablifhment. It is not merely that the church
would, but that the whole conftitution would,
be endangered by an unlimited admiffion of
Diffenters

Diffenters of every denomination into offices of power and truft. If Sir William Meredith's letter is a true reprefentation of their principles, they are for a conftitution wherein they might feel their own importance, and ftrut and fwagger over a king of ftraw, and if thefe are their principles they doubtlefs would not reft under any other; confequently the gratifying them in the repeal of the Teft laws, as it would certainly make a breach in the conftitution, fo would it as certainly tend to the total fubverfion of it. Wifely, therefore, moft wifely did the minifter prefs the danger arifing from innovation, and it is hoped that a dread of that danger will at all times be deeply imprefled upon the mind of every fenator.

Innovations in the ftate are never to be attempted under a profpect of a probable good. They are to be attempted only where there is a moral certainty that good will, and that evil will not, be the confequence of them. Nothing is to be rifked or hazarded. If there is danger in the projected innovation; if there is no certainty, only a chance, that good will be derived from it, it is a fufficient objection to its being attempted. At the Revolution there was a moral certainty of good in the prefervation of our religion and liberties. Nothing was rifked or hazarded; for had we
failed

failed in effecting the revolution we should
have been but where we were before, under the
bigotted rule of James, supported by his friends
the Diffenters. But for what should any innovating enterprife be undertaken now? Our
liberties are all defined ; and under our moft
defervedly and much beloved king we are in
the full enjoyment of them. Our religion is
unmolefted, and we are free in the exercife
of all its facred functions. All the feveral
diffenters of every denomination from the religion of the conftitution, are all amply tolerated and unreftrained in the exercife of theirs.
Our conftitution, if perhaps the keen eye of
the philofophical ftatefman can difcern fome
little imperfection in any part of it, and nothing human is perfect, what man of a found
underftanding and a found and good heart,
would wifh that any rifk should be run in an
attempt to remove it ; and more efpecially
when that imperfection may be rather faid
to be difcoverable than felt ? But with regard to the Diffenters, our conftitution hath
nothing of imperfection even difcoverable in
it, unlefs indeed any man chufes to call it
fuch that they are admitted to have a feat in
the Houfe of Commons. The Teft laws are
no blemifh to it, nor if removed would they
add any thing to its ftrength or excellence.
How would the conftitution shine with greater
fplendor

fplendor becaufe a diffenter might be a Tidewaiter or an Excifeman? which from the
pamphlet under confideration, one would
imagine was the only reafon why the Writer
wiſhes the Teſt to be removed. But this,
your Lordſhip will be pleafed to obſerve, is a
piece of diffenter craft; he mentions only the
loweſt offices, but hath his eye ſteadily fixed
upon the higheſt, well knowing that if the
one was open to them, it would not be long
before they would take poffeffion of the other.
It is not for the fake of a Tidewaiter's or
Excifeman's place that they wifh the Teſt to
be removed, but for fomething more refpeet-
able. However, be it for the one or the other,
thefe offices ſtand in no need of affiſtance from
the Diffenters, being very well filled and ex-
ecuted by members of the conſtitution; and
therefore any innovation for the fake of admitting the diffenters to offices for which
they are not at all wanted, cannot but be
confidered as extremely unneceffary and im-
politic, and in the end would prove injurious
to the conſtitution in the higheſt degree.

It does not appear by any thing which the
Writer of your Lordſhip's admired pamphlet
hath faid, that any particular advantage would
accrue to the conſtitution from the repeal of
the Teſt, and the admiffion of Diffenters to
offices of truſt. The advantages which he

either

either enumerates or refers to are all such as
would accrue to the Diffenters only.

It is true he wishes us to think that no
harm can arise to the conftitution from the admiffion of the Diffenters. That other countries have made the experiment, and, unfortunately for his argument, p. 81. that the
" Court of France had within thefe few years
raifed M. Neckar to the head of the finances."
Moft unfortunately urged indeed ! However,
we will not dwell upon it, nor upon the piti-
able and diftracted ftate of France, with Mr.
Neckar at the head of its finances. But, notwithftanding this plain evidence to the contrary, let us allow in its fulleft fcope all that
he contends for. That other countries had
tried the experiment, and that no harm had
arifen from it. Yet how does this apply to us?
The Englifh conftitution does not prevail in
thefe other countries, nor in any other country upon the globe, that we are acquainted
with. And except it did prevail where the
experiment had been tried with fuccefs, the argument is good for nothing. It is the ftrength,
the prefervation, nay, it is effential to the Englifh conftitution, that Diffenters from its
principle fhould not be admitted to the adminiftration of its offices; *becaufe, if admitted,
there is no check provided for preventing them
when in office from totally overthrowing it.* Let
the

the Layman, or any other for him, difprove this if he can.

It is obfervable alfo that in the heterogeneous mafs of arguments, new vampt from *Tindall*, &c. which he makes ufe of, and which have been anfwered an hundred times, he makes the repeal of the teft laws to be a matter in which the Church and the Clergy only would be concerned; and ftates things as if the lay members of the conftitution had nothing at all to do with it; whereas the Layman is as much concerned in it as the Ecclefiaftic; for when the conftitution is laid in ruins, it is not merely the Ecclefiaftic, but men of every defcription in the conftitution that would be the fufferers: therefore thofe perfons who have been over perfuaded into a favourable opinion of the repeal of the Teft laws, ought to reconfider the matter. Revolutions, even when neceffity obliges us, are neverthelefs dreadful inftruments to have recourfe to, and during the competition for them it is impoffible to fay who has moft at ftake. This man in his threat and fuggeftion, p. 60, intimates that the Ecclefiaftic has. But the fatal event of 1648, and the confufions preceding and fubfequent to it, plainly fhewed that it is not only the intereft of the Ecclefiaftic that is concerned in the prefervation of

C   the

the conftitution, but of the whole commū-
nity.

If it be afked why offices and places of
truft are limited only to perfons profef-
fing the religion of the eftablifhment, the anfwer is : The religion of the eftablifhment
being fo admirably adapted to the fupport
of the conftitution, being fo diftant from
any poffibility of bringing injury or incon-
venience to it, and other religions of thofe
that are known to us, be their excellence in
other refpects what it may, maintaining principles with which it is impoffible the conftitution can confift ; it is therefore provided
by the excellent wifdom of the laws, that no
perfons but fuch as profefs the religion of the
eftablifhment fhall be admitted to offices or
places of truft. It is not that their creeds or
modes of worfhip, but the principles with
regard to government which accompany
them, that render perfons of this defcription
incompetent to offices or places of truft. In
other refpects thefe perfons may be as worthy
and refpectable characters as members of the
eftablifhment, but in the principle that ac-
companies their religion it is impoffible they
can be well wifhers to or hearty fupporters
of the conftitution ; therefore as it is the object of the laws to preferve the conftitution

as

as it is at prefent in its beautiful blendings into one whole of the feveral known forms of human government, wifely is it provided that the adminiftration of government in all its offices fhall be by thofe whofe principles (by profeffion at leaft) fhall be confiftent with its prefervation. Such are the principles which naturally accompany the religion of the eftablifhment, and therefore is it required that all who bear offices in the conftitution fhall be profeffed members of the eftablifh-ment. Hence the Teft laws are to be confi-dered, not as religious tefts, but as tefts of principle with regard to the conftitution, and when confidered in this their true light, he muft have either a very weak judgement, or be very unfriendly to the conftitution, who wifhes their repeal.

One general error pervading the whole of the pamphlet under confideration (and it is to be fuppofed not an involuntary one) is, that the Teft laws are confidered as tefts of religion, and that they were enacted merely with a view to the prefervation of the efta-blifhed church. This is extremely falfe and unjuft, for the principal object in the firft framing of thefe laws, even in their very origin, was the prefervation of the *ftate* from being again reduced under the tyranny

of

of the Bifhop of Rome, and their relation to
the church was no otherwife than as the
church was incorporated into the ftate. It
is the fame now as then, and thefe laws as
in their firft intention are to operate for the
prefervation of the conftitution from being
reduced under any tyranny, whether lay or
ecclefiaftical, whether of one or of many;
and therefore he who truly is a friend to the
conftitution as it is at prefent, and fincerely
wifhes its continuance, never can confiftently
with that wifh give his vote for the repeal of
the Teft laws.

Would you, if you are a friend to the
conftitution, admit to the adminiftration of
its government perfons who you know are
by principle not well-wifhers to it, who
would change or overthrow it if they could?
Muft not a man be wonderfully deranged in
his judgment that would do this ? It is not
merely on account of the fuperior excellence
of the religion of the eftablifhment as a religion ? it is not for the purpofe of gaining
profelytes to it from other religions that the
Teft laws are framed ? but it is for the purpofe of continuing and preferving the conftitution as it is at prefent, which whoever
wifhes to have continued to us cannot confiftently defire the Teft laws to be repealed.

Sir

Sir William Meredith fays, the " Romifh " religion is not bad for fociety on account " of its fuperftition, but the doctrines it " maintains with regard to civil power." The fame is applicable to the Prefbyterians, who by principle are profeffedly Republicans, and who of courfe never would concur to fupport a government that was not Repub- lican. The Quaker, the Anabaptift, the Independents in general are all of a levelling principle, enemies to all diftinctions of rank or orders. How is it poffible fuch perfons could contribute to the fupport of a confti- tution which is throughout fo beautifully va- riegated by its gradual and regular fubordi- nations, and which muft neceffarily ceafe to be if its inequalities were levelled. In a word, if the Teft laws fhould be repealed the con- ftitution cannot poffibly long continue to be what it is at prefent, it will unavoidably be overwhelmed by that inundation of oppofite and difcordant opinions which would then rufh into the offices of ftate, and terminate only in anarchy and confufion.

Let it be once more repeated, that the conftitution, as it at prefent is framed from the blending together of the Hierarchical, Monarchical, Ariftocratical, and Democra- tical forms of government, that with a con-

ftitution

ftitution thus framed none will agree who by the principle of their religion are attached only to one of the forms of which it is compounded, that therefore it is neceffary even to the exiftence of the prefent conftitution, that its offices fhould be adminiftered only by thofe who from principle are friends to it, and whofe religion depends upon the prefervation of the conftitution; and therefore he that wifhes to preferve it cannot confiftently vote for the repeal of the Teft laws; becaufe if he does he muft neceffarily vote for the deftruction of that which at the fame time he wifhes fhould be preferved.

As it is not intended to detain your Lordfhip with a long letter, and much lefs with fuch a length of fcribble as that of your friend the Layman, let us haften to a conclufion, previoufly obferving on that very nugatory pretence for repealing the Teft, which is derived from the profanation of the facrament by occafional conformity.

The occafional conformift it muft be acknowledged certainly doth profane the facrament; and therefore—what?—therefore the Teft laws ought to be repealed, fay the Diffenters and your Lordfhip's friend, and then there could be no occafional conformity. True,

True, my Lord, there could not, but then by a parity of reafoning the Ten commandments ought to be repealed, and then there could be no tranfgreffion of them; by a parity of reafoning oaths fhould be abolifhed, and then there would be no perjury. It is at the peril of the occafional conformift if he profanes the facrament, but the law which requires evidence of the principles of perfons employed in the ftate, is not the caufe of the profanation any more than the law requiring an oath to be taken is the caufe of the perjury which may follow. If your Lordfhip, or Lordfhip's friend for you, can prove that government hath no right to require evidence of the principles of thofe whom it employs you will do fomething, but till you have or can do this all arguments drawn from the profanation of the facred rite by the occafional conformift are childifh and nugatory in the extreme.

The conclufion from the foregoing obfervations is, that the pamphlet fo ftrongly recommended by your Lordfhip is not what you have reprefented it to be. That the principle of it is faulty, as there can be no *right* to a toleration, and much lefs a right for perfons to enjoy the privileges of a fociety of which they are not truly members.

That

That the Teft laws do not refpect the church
in particular but the whole conftitution; that
the teft is not a teft only of the religion a
perfon may profefs, its object is to difcover
the principle of the perfon, whether friendly
or hoftile to the conftitution, the merit of
his religion, as a religion is totally out of
the queftion; that the confequence of the
teft is not an exclufion from office, on account of creeds or modes of worfhip, and
therefore that the Teft laws are not perfecuting, nor the Diffenters, as this writer reprefents, perfecuted.

Every ftate hath indifputably within itfelf a right to require evidence of the principles of thofe whom it employs, and
whether they are friendly or hoftile. It
hath alfo as certainly a right of determining
what fhall or fhall not be deemed fuch evidence. Availing itfelf of fuch right the
ftate hath required that all perfons employed
in offices under it, fhall within a limited time
receive the facrament of the Lord's Supper,
according to the ufage of the Church of
England, and they who refufe to comply
with fuch requifition are adjudged to hold
principles unfriendly to the conftitution.
Where now, in the exercife of this un-
doubted right, is the perfecution of the
Dif-

Diffenters ? No where, my Lord, it is a right fully authorifed by all the known laws of juftice, equity, and right reafon, with which the world hath at any time been made acquainted.

There is one moft curious argument which your friend hath urged for the abolition of the Teft, and hath been overlooked in the fore-going obfervations. It is this : " that the " Teft was originally framed againft the Pa-" pifts, at a time when there were no Dif-" fenters, and that therefore it ought not to " operate againft the Diffenters." This re-doubted argument fhall be anfwered by the following fhort apologue : A farmer who had frequently been plundered in his poultry-yard by the foxes, whom he could by no art or ftratagem circumvent, after fome thought contrived a fence which would for ever keep them off from coming any where upon his premifes. There were at this time no other beafts or vermin in the country that were at all troublefome to him. In procefs of time, however, the wolves came into his neighbourhood, and the fence proving a fuf-ficient barrier againft them alfo, an old wolf took an opportunity of accofting the farmer, and requefting him to admit him and his comrades to come upon his premifes, for that

it

it was a great hardfhip upon them to be thus fhut out. The fence, fays he, you well know, was never originally intended againft us, for we were not in the country when you raifed it; and befides we are as great enemies to the foxes as you can be, and with our affiftance, were the fence entirely thrown down, you would need be under no apprehenfion from them. What you fay, Mr. Wolf, replies the farmer, is in a great meafure true; the fence originally was certainly not intended againft you, and I can well believe that you are as great an enemy to the foxes as I myfelf am; but as you are as great an enemy to me as you are to the foxes, with your good leave the fence fhall continue juft as it is, and I am happy to find that it anfwers the double purpofe of keeping out the wolves as effectually as it does the foxes.

And now, my Lord, having done with the pamphlet, fuffer a few words to be addreffed to your Lordfhip and your friends in particular; and they are to requeft you to look, to reflect upon the Englifh conftitution, and then fay where upon earth you can find greater or even equal excellence; regular in its formation, mild in its operations, friendly, benevolent to all, anxious

ious only for its own prefervation, and this
anxiety expreffed not by any unjuft, op-
preffive, or perfecuting meafures, but by
thofe wife and prudent ones which every
houfeholder adopts for the prefervation of
himfelf and his family, who would be con-
demned as a miferable manager if he was to
admit into his fervice perfons who were
known to be enemies to his domeftic ar-
rangements and œconomy. Such, and fuch
only is the anxiety expreffed by the conftitution for its own prefervation ; and therefore
in fuch expreffion of it, in the eyes of all
wife and experienced perfons is it altogether
irreprehenfible; and as it is irreprehenfible in
this, fo likewife is it moft truly admirable in
the happinefs of its temperament and the
happinefs which we all enjoy under it.   Our
kings fhine with the fplendour of Eaftern
monarchs, but without any of their terrific
powers ; gently are they coerced without
violence or difrefpect, and their throne is eftablifhed by the freedom of thofe over whom
they reign.   The fubject likewife hath all
the happinefs that he is capable of in a
ftate of fociety, and if he is reftrained from
licentioufnefs, ftill is he not abridged of his
liberty, and knows no controul but the controul of the laws.   Such then being the

bleffings

of our moſt excellent conſtitution, where is
the heart that doth not vibrate in uniſon with
the prayer?—O preſerve it Heaven!—Let
us lay aſide then, my Lord, all thoſe little
party cabals, thoſe factious doings, the
marks of children rather than of men, of
which we have heard ſo much of late. If
we are men of ambition let us diſplay that
true nobleneſs of ſoul which• ſaith, it is
better that my ambition ſhould be diſap-
pointed, than that the conſtitution ſhould be
overthrown. If we have been treated with
indignity by any particular individuals let us
not, for the ſake of gratifying a poor deſpi-
cable reſentment, hazard the introduction of
a general fire and confuſion, but with a firm
ſtedfaſtneſs, which will do us honour, let
us repreſs our reſentment within its proper
limits; or if it muſt be gratified, let us gra-
tify it without acting like madmen. In a
word let no views of party ambition or reſentment operate upon us; let no hopes of
bettering our fortune, or of being relieved
from our domeſtic neceſſities, induce us to
riſk, to hazard any thing which may even
by a caſual contingency endanger the conſtitution; but let it be our pride, as aſſuredly
it is our intereſt, ever to preſerve it invi-
olate.

And

And with regard to you, my Lord, it is recommended to you to perfevere induftrioufly in your ftudies, that you may again inftruct the Bifhops in religion; teach again law to the Lord Chancellor: carefully, moreover, endeavouring to improve yourfelf in the feveral manœuvres of the Cleft Stick, whereby fo much ftrength, as by the various exertions of your arms and body, fo much grace is added to the throws of your Lordfhip's oratory.

I have the honour to be, my Lord,

Your very humble Servant.